This book is dedicated
to all the soldiers who
have been called away
from their families
to preserve the
peace and freedom
of the United States
of America.

A special thank you to:

My editors, Dorina K. Lazo
and Virginia Hergenroeder
My mother, Frankie Kalmanir
My children and inspiration,
T.J. and Kamila
My best friend and husband,
James
and all the others who have
encouraged me and believed
in the creation of this project.

The story, "Daddy Got His Orders", is an imprint of T.J. Publishing Co.
Published by T.J. Publishing Co.
1099 E. Champlain, Suite A #152,
Fresno, CA 93720
Copyright © 2004 Kathy Mitchell
Fresno, California
Printed in Hong Kong

10 9 8 7 6 5 4 3 2 1

Library of Congress Control Number: 2004096573
Kathy Mitchell
The story of "Daddy Got His Orders" / written by Kathy Mitchell
Illustrated by Ernie "Hergie" Hergenroeder
Summary: The story of a child whose father must leave for military service
and how he prepares for his father's extended absence.
ISBN: 0-9760811-0-5 (Hardcover)
Copyright to include all characters, design & story concept.

DADDY
GOT HIS ORDERS

Written by.
Kathy Mitchell

Illustrated by:
Ernie Hergenroeder
HERGIE

One peaceful afternoon. . .

1

T.J., Mommy and his sister, Kamila, put a sign up on their garage door that said, "PRAY FOR OUR DADDY." They tied a yellow ribbon around the mailbox.

T.J. asked Mommy, "Why are we decorating our house when no one else is?"

Later, Mommy explained to T.J.,

"Honey, Daddy got his orders.
He has to go now to protect our country."

T.J. asked, *"Why is Daddy going to fight for the country?*
To protect us? Because he loves us?"

His mommy assured him,
"Yes Dear, Daddy loves us very much."

"But who will protect Daddy?" asked T.J.

"God will protect Daddy and all the other soldiers like Daddy.
He could not be in better hands," said Mommy.

*"Mommy, I want to be a soldier just like Daddy.
I want to fight for our country," said T.J.
"I am going to join the Army!"*

"I can even fit into Daddy's duffel bag."
"Son, you are only 5; you have to be at least 17 to join the Army.
Besides, Mommy needs you here at home." "OK, Mommy, but if Daddy
is going to fight the enemy, could the enemy win and Daddy lose?"
"Yes, T.J., that is possible, but remember who is watching over your Daddy."

T.J. knew he needed to help Mommy at home but he still wanted to know how long Daddy would be gone. *"Will he be here for my birthday? For Christmas?"*

"No, Son, he will be gone for over a year."

T.J. asked, *"Will Daddy be here for his birthday? Will he have a cake with candles to blow out? Who will give him presents?"*

*"He **has** to have his birthday!"*

*"Honey, he will have a birthday,
but he will not be able to be here with us," said Mommy.*

*"Yes he will, Mommy. You see, Daddy is right here in my heart forever.
Whenever I miss Daddy, I just give myself a hug and I am hugging him, too.
Daddy can never leave my heart."*

The next day when T.J. left for school with Daddy in his heart, he told his friends that Daddy got his orders and had to leave.

The teacher opened class by saying the Pledge of Allegiance.
T.J. knew every word as he stared at the American flag.
All the other kids did, too, because they knew that
T.J.'s dad was going to serve the country.
T.J. didn't know what the stars and stripes meant but he did
know that Daddy wore that same flag on his uniform.

When T.J. came home from school, he wanted to talk to his Daddy.
He knew that he could use the computer to send messages or pictures to him.
There might even be one waiting for him from Daddy on the computer.

He asked Mommy to use one of his funny face pictures to e-mail to Daddy. T.J. wanted to make him laugh.

Daddy e-mailed back to the family what he missed from home: fly swatters, yummy snacks, his favorite songs and batteries. He asked for some hard candies to share with the children in that country. Of course, what Daddy wished for the most was to hug his family. He told T.J. to take care of Mommy and Sissy and that he loves them very much.

Mommy, Sissy and T.J. began putting together
a care package for Daddy.
T.J. ran to the laundryroom.
" Don't forget the fly swatter Daddy asked for! " said T.J.
" Thank you T.J., that will make Daddy happy," said Mommy.

That night Mommy tucked T.J. in bed
and read him his two favorite bedtime stories. This time the stories made
him sad because they were about kids with their mommys and daddys.
His daddy wasn't there.
Then Mommy reminded him to say his prayers.

"*Dear God, please bless my entire family...
my mommy, my sister, my grandma, my grandpa
and, **especially**, bless my Daddy.
I know we will be safe because Daddy is protecting the country.
I know he will be safe because you are protecting him.
Amen.*"